NORMAL PUBLIC LIBRARY

A12005 414237

W9-CKI-279

NORMAL PUBLIC LIBRARY
206 W. COLLEGE AVE.
NORMAL, IL 61761

DEMCO

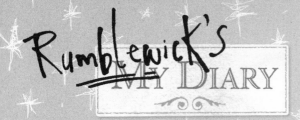

Rumblewick's ~~My~~ DIARY

My Unwilling Witch Sleeps Over

Hiawyn Oram • Sarah Warburton

NORMAL PUBLIC LIBRARY
NORMAL, ILLINOIS 61761

LITTLE, BROWN AND COMPANY
Books for Young Readers
New York Boston

To Giselle and Nicola,
for being so incredibly good
H. O.

For Lizzie
S. W.

Text copyright © 2007 by Hiawyn Oram
Illustrations copyright © 2007 by Sarah Warburton

All rights reserved. Except as permitted under the U.S. Copyright Act of 1976,
no part of this publication may be reproduced, distributed, or transmitted in any form
or by any means, or stored in a database or retrieval system, without the prior
written permission of the publisher.

Little, Brown Books for Young Readers

Hachette Book Group
237 Park Avenue, New York, NY 10017
Visit our Web site at www.lb-kids.com

Little, Brown Books for Young Readers is a division of Hachette Book Group,
Inc. The Little, Brown name and logo are trademarks of Hachette Book Group, Inc.

First U.S. Edition: May 2009
First published in Great Britain in 2007 by Orchard Books

The characters and events portrayed in this book are fictitious. Any similarity to real
persons, living or dead, is coincidental and not intended by the author.

Library of Congress Cataloging-in-Publication Data

Oram, Hiawyn.
My unwilling witch sleeps over / by Hiawyn Oram ; illustrated by Sarah Warburton. —1st
U.S. ed.
p. cm. — (Rumblewick's diary ; #2)
Summary: Much to Rumblewick's dismay, his reluctant witch befriends a couple of Otherside
girls and begins to go to sleepovers.
ISBN 978-0-316-03453-1
[1. Witches—Fiction. 2. Cats—Fiction. 3. Sleepovers—Fiction. 4. Diaries—Fiction. 5.
Humorous stories.] I. Warburton, Sarah, ill. II. Title.
PZ7.0624Ms 2009
[Fic]—dc22
2009000202

10 9 8 7 6 5 4 3 2 1

RRD-C

Printed in the United States of America

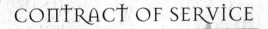

CONTRACT OF SERVICE

between
WITCH HAGATHA AGATHA, Haggy Aggy for short, HA for shortest
of Thirteen Chimneys, Wizton-under-Wold

&

the Witch's Familiar,
RUMBLEWICK SPELLWACKER MORTIMER B, RB for short

It is hereby agreed that, come
FIRE, Brimstone, CAULDRONS overflowing,
or ALIEN WIZARDS invading,
for the NEXT SEVEN YEARS
RB will serve HA,
obey her EVERY WHIM AND WORD and at all times assist her
in the ways of being a true and proper WITCH.

PAYMENT for services will be:
* a log basket to sleep in * unlimited slime buns for breakfast
* free use of HA's broomsticks (outside of peak brooming hours)
* and a cracked mirror for luck.

PENALTY for failing in his duties will be decided on the whim of
THE HAGS on HIGH.

SIGNED AND SEALED
this New Moon Day, 22nd of Remember

Haggy Aggy
....
Witch Hagatha Agatha

Rumblewick

Rumblewick Spellwacker Mortimer B

Trixie Fiddlestick

And witnessed by the High Hag Trixie Fiddlestick

A SHORT HISTORY
OF HOW YOU COME TO BE READING MY
VERY PRIVATE DIARIES

In a snail shell, they were STOLEN. Oh yes, no less. My witch, Haggy Aggy (HA for short), sneaked into my log basket and helped herself.

According to her, this is what happened:

On one of her many shopping trips to Your Side she met a Book Wiz. (I am told you call them publishers, though Wiz seems more fitting as they make books appear, as if by magic, every day of the week.)

Anyway, this Book Wiz/publisher wanted HA to write an account of HER life as a witch here on Our Side. Of course, HA wasn't willing to do that. Being the most unwilling witch in witchdom, she is far too busy shopping, watching TV, not cackling, being anything BUT a witch, and getting me into trouble with the High Hags* as a result.

The Book Wiz begged on her knees (apparently) and offered HA a life's supply of shoes if she came up with something. So HA did. She came up with THIS — MY DIARIES. ALL OF THEM!!!!

Of course, when I wrote the diaries, I was not expecting anyone to read them. Let alone Othersiders like you. But as you are, here is a word to the wise about how things work between us:

* The High Hags run everything around here. They RULE.

1. We are here on THIS SIDE and you are there on the OTHER SIDE.

2. Between us is the HORIZON LINE.

3. You don't see we're here, on This Side, living our lives, because for you the Horizon Line is always a day away. You can walk for a thousand moons (or more for all I know), but you'll never reach it.

4. On the other paw, we know you're there because we visit you all the time. This is partly because of broomsticks. A broomstick has no trouble with any Horizon Line anywhere. A broomstick (with one or more of us upon it) just flies straight through.

And it has to be like that because scaring Otherside children into their wits is part of witches' work. In fact it is Number One on the Witches' Charter of Good Practice (see copy glued at the back).

On the other paw, it is NOWHERE in the Charter for a witch to go over to Your Side to make friends and try to be and do everything you are and do — as my witch, Haggy Aggy, does.

But then, that's my giant problem: being cat to a witch who doesn't want to be one. And as you will see from these diaries, it makes my life a right BAG OF HEDGEHOGS. So all I can say is, if HA tries to make friends with YOU, send her straight back to This Side with a spider in her ear.

Thank you,

Rumblewick Spellwacker Mortimer B. xxx

THIS DIARY BELONGS TO:

Rumblewick Spellwacker Mortimer B.

RUMBLEWICK for short, RB for shortest

ADDRESS:
Thirteen Chimneys,
Wizton-under-Wold, This Side
Bird's Eye View: 331 N by WW

TELEPHONE:
77+3-5+1-7

NEAREST OTHERSIDE TELEPHONE:
Ditch and Candleberry Bush Street,
N by SE Over the Horizon

BIRTHDAY:
Windy Day 23rd Magogary

EDUCATION:
The Awethunder School for Familiars
12-Moon Apprenticeship to the
High Hag Witch Trixie Fiddlestick

QUALIFICATIONS:
Certified Witch's Familiar

CURRENT EMPLOYMENT:
Seven-year contract with Witch Hagatha Agatha,
Haggy Aggy for short, HA for shortest

HOBBIES:
Catnastics, Point-to-Point Shrewing, Languages

NEXT OF KIN:
Uncle Sherbet (retired Witch's Familiar)
Moldy Old Cottage,
Flying Teapot Street,
Prancetown

Foggy Night in the Far Quagmires

Dear Diary,

Sorry if this looks skew-wiggle. We're sleeping over at Haggy Aggy's aunt's in the Far Quagmires — and I'm writing under the spare bed, by the light of a tired firefly.

We only came for our usual once-a-moon drop-in. But then the fog came down and Pondernot (HA's aunt) wouldn't let us fly home in it.

Haggy Aggy is in the bed, tossing and turning so hard, she's sending the mattress straw flying — all over me and all over you. I'm certain she's sleeping so badly on purpose — as a protest — because she doesn't want to be here.

And I can sympathize with that.

Pondernot is a bent little witch with rosy cheeks.

To look at her you'd think she couldn't bring a brew to a bubble in a boiling cauldron.

But one thing is certainly boiling about her: only she, in the whole universe, is able to make HA feel RUBBLEROT about not being a more willing witch.

And this visit, thanks to her snooping Familiar —

Sassy
Elevenlives
Selfright —

there's been more than usual to make HA feel RUBBLEROT about

Apparently last Ghastly night, Sassy the Snoop "just happened" to drop in to the Deep Ditch in Wizton — a favorite Familiars' haunt.

While she was there, it "just happened" that the High Hags' Familiars came in.

(Well, surprise, surprise, as everyone knows they always go to the Deep Ditch on Ghastly night.)

3

It also "just happened" that their tattlechat was all about HA and how their Hags suspect she's trying to become less of a witch and more of an Othersider with every moon that passes.

I can imagine the Snoop couldn't get home fast enough to tell Pondernot. And, furnished with this information, Pondernot has been making HA feel like complete GRUBSPIT.

Not by harrying and pointing her pointing finger. She never does that. But by getting under HA's skin with sharp little needles of "deep disappointment." Somehow making HA feel GUILTY for getting HER a bad reputation by association.

Now, while on the one paw
I wish I had Pondernot's ability to do this,
on the other I'm glad I do not.

For one good reason: feeling
guilty does not suit Haggy Aggy.
It puts her in a mood so dark it's as if
she's under a personal eclipse of the sun
and moon and can't see her own foot
in front of her.

Back at Thirteen Chimneys after Getting Lost and Diverted by the JIM

Dear Diary,

We're home, thank the stars. Back from the Far Quagmires, though by no means out of the "quagmire."

To continue: what with the grubspit feelings of guilt and having to sleep over — by the time the fog lifted and we came to leave Pondernot's — HA's mood was so dark she could hardly see her way out of the front door.

Though I was standing there ready with our broomstick, she walked straight past me and nearly fell into one of the bog fires in what Pondernot fondly calls her

"garden."

This put HA
into an even fouler
mood. Followed by an even
fouler one, when Pondernot said
with a crooked smile, "Now, my
dear, you know how much it would
upset me to see a fully fledged witch
being flown by her Familiar. So I hope
you'll be flying that broomstick home
yourself as any AUNT-RESPECTING
witch would do."

With a thundery snarl, HA grabbed
our broomstick, mounted it, and
took off with barely time for
me to leap on behind.

Well, the truth is, Diary, in the dark
mood she was in, HA should <u>NOT</u> have been
flying anything, anywhere. Let alone from the
Far Quagmires to Wizton-under-Wold.
It requires much alertness of the stars above
and landmarks below. It should <u>NEVER</u> be
attempted by one in a personal eclipse and
hardly able to see
    her own flying hand
              in front of her.

11

So, inevitably, in spite of my attempts to navigate from the back of the broom,

WE WENT THE <u>WRONG</u> <u>WAY</u>.

We went so wrong, we ended up crossing the Horizon and flying uselessly hither and thither on the Other Side, until HA said she was feeling so sick she was going to fall off.

I took my life in my paws, clung and clawed my way past her to take over the flying, and quickly brought us down — as I thought safely — on

the nearest suitable landing place.

As it turned out, it wasn't safe or suitable.

It was the roof of a building in which, HA was soon to discover, Otherside children go to do JIM (similar to catnastics, if a clumsier version).

And now that we were off-broomstick and away from guilt and the Far Quagmires, HA's dark mood suddenly lifted.

NORMAL PUBLIC LIBRARY
NORMAL, ILLINOIS 61761

Her sun and moon came out again.

She dangled cheerfully from the water pipes of the building, so she could peer in and eavesdrop at a half-open window.

"Oh, RB," she cried, "do take a look.

"There are darling girls in there doing what they call 'JIM' — leaping, tumbling, propelling, and turning free through the air. No springs on their feet, no wings on their shoulders! Oh, how I'd love to be what they be and do what they do. And do you know what? Because I would love to,

I've decided I will!"

Well, you know Haggy Aggy. Once she's decided, she's decided.
So forget Pondernot's guiltifyings about being more Other Side than This Side.
An Otherside JIM girl is what HA is going to _be_!!

15

I mean, we've only been home five tads of tell and she's already turned herself into a JIM Girl Lookalike.

And magicked up a JIM bag full of JIM wear so tomorrow she can join the "darling JIM girls" in their <u>JIMMY</u> activities.

She is in her room now, trying out a spell she made me invent the moment we came in the door — namely

The Triple-Turn-in-Air-
without-Landing-in-
a-Complete-Splat spell.

I don't know how but I've got to keep this from the tattlechat at the Deep Ditch.

Imagine if Sassy the Snoop hears of it and informs Aunt Pondernot?

All I can say is, dark moodwise,

better not ponder it!

16

JIM Day the First Night

Dear Diary,

Talk about being exhausted. I've had to spend all afternoon in that JIM building tucked down in HA's JIM bag,

OBSERVING AND LEARNING
SO AS TO HELP HER
BECOME A GREAT JIMMER."

And then, since we got home, I've had to invent four more spells, "using what I've observed and learned."

<u>All</u>, please note, when I was supposed to be somewhere quite else — at practice for

the Grand Steeplechase Race!!

More of that later.

For now, here are all five spells (which she's asked me to set in a booklet she can tuck into her JIM pants for easy reference).

Spell 1

THE TRIPLE-TURN-IN-AIR-WITHOUT-LANDING-IN-A-COMPLETE-SPLAT SPELL

Tuck yourself up tight as a catkin bud in a witch's hat and chant:

My feet are sprung like springy springs
My feet so sprung will give me wings
And stepping from this witch's hat
I'll fly up from the gymnast's mat
And in a wondrous sky-high bound
I'll have the time to turn me round
Not once, not twice, but three times over
Then land as if I land in CLOVER.

Spell 2

THE FLY-OVER-
THE-HORSE SPELL

Make your broomstick invisible using any
reliable Invisible Broomstick spell.
Lie on "the horse" and chant with authority:

You are no longer lifeless
You are a living horse
As vaulting you I must be
You'll help me in my course
And as I come a-flying
You'll be there for my hands
While making very, very sure
You're NOT there when I lands.

Spell 3

THE GLUED-ON-A-BEAM SPELL

Mix one dollop spider's web jam, one dollop burr jelly, one dollop pine tree goo. Just before you mount the balance beam, apply mixture to soles of your shoes or feet and chant:

I will stay, I will stick
I will never stumble
See my feet return so neat
From each leap and tumble
I'm so stable, I'm so able
I can make the team
I am glued on like I'm screwed on —
TO THIS BALANCE BEAM.

Spell 4

THE NO-HANDS-SWING-BARS SPELL

When called to mount the bars, twirl on your left foot backwards seven times while chanting inwardly:

I am so sure between these bars
I circle, swing, release
It seems I am a Spinning Wheel
My speed I don't decrease.
I am supreme between these bars
I hardly need them there
One giant swing and look — no hands — I am at home in air

Spell 5

THE ELEVENTEEN-TUMBLES-IN-A-ROW SPELL

Sprinkle yourself liberally with
sawdust eleventeen times, and
on the eleventeenth shout:

Eleventeen tumbles in a row
Here I go, here I go.
Nothing can stop me,
No one can top me
I'm the One-Witch-Girl-
Tumble Show!

Not bad, given I've only been
acquainted with JIM for

SOCKS, SOCKS,

TADPOLES IN SOCKS!

What's going on. The whole house is
shaking. Is it the end of the universe? Be
back when I've found out

Dear Diary,

Sorry to keep you in suspense. It wasn't the end of the universe or even Wizton-under-Wold.

Apparently, at JIM, HA made friends with two JIM GIRLS named Zinnia and Tulip. They've invited her for a shake at a nearby Shake Shop after JIMMING tomorrow.

<u>So</u>, because HA always has to be the best at everything (except being a proper witch), she has been practicing her shake.

Well, I hope they don't invite her every day.

I mean, look at this place! I'll be working till dawn unshaking it.

HA Gets an Even Worse
Invitation Day Night

Dear Diary

Can you believe this? HA got it all wrong. A Shake Shop is not a place you go to shake yourself till the universe trembles. It is a kind of Gatheria where you meet with your friends — to slurp googuff through hollow reeds called straws.

When HA discovered this, she picked up her JIM bag (me in it) and rushed to the Shake Shop bathroom. Here, she had the nerve to give me an ear-wigging!

"Why didn't you <u>TELL</u> me a shake is a drink?" she hissed as she wigged one ear.

"Because I had no idea!" I hissed back.

"Well, why didn't you? You're my Familiar. You're supposed to be Othersidewise," she wigged the other ear.

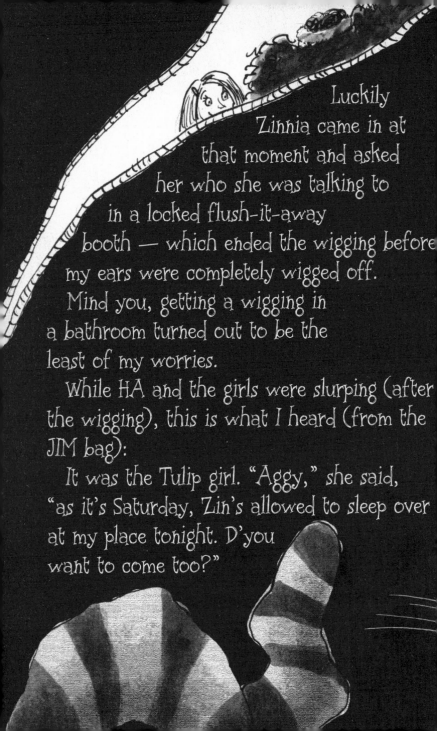

Luckily Zinnia came in at that moment and asked her who she was talking to in a locked flush-it-away booth — which ended the wigging before my ears were completely wigged off.

Mind you, getting a wigging in a bathroom turned out to be the least of my worries.

While HA and the girls were slurping (after the wigging), this is what I heard (from the JIM bag):

It was the Tulip girl. "Aggy," she said, "as it's Saturday, Zin's allowed to sleep over at my place tonight. D'you want to come too?"

Well, I nearly jumped out of the bag onto Tulip's lap to tell her

NO, UNDER NO CIRCUMSTANCES CAN "AGGY" SLEEP ANYWHERE TONIGHT. IT IS THE HEATS OF THE WITCH'S CAT STEEPLECHASE AND SHE HAS TO BE THERE TO VOUCH FOR ME OR I WILL NOT BE ALLOWED TO ENTER!

Somehow I held myself back, only to hear HA say in a cooey voice:

"Oh, Tulip,
        that is SWEET of you.

Normally I don't like sleeping over.

    But if you mean wearing

a pink nightgown and watching TV

    all night on your sofa,

            then I should think so!"

At this Zinnia giggled and Tulip said, "Yes, though Zin and I wear jimjams. They're better for bouncing in. And don't forget your toothbrush because my mom makes us brush our teeth, even though she knows we have a midnight feast afterward.

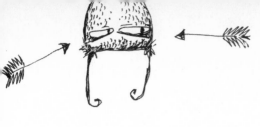

So if you want to come, here's my address."

Well, when we left that Shake Shop, HA started screeching with excitement.

"I'm going to sleep over!

With Zin and Tu!

And meet a MOM.

And be told to brush my teeth

before a midnight feast!

Oh I'm so excited, I could fly!"

I was SO embarrassed — there were passersby — but there was no time for that. I had to get her home triple-presto and talk some sense into her head about the importance of the Steeplechase Heats.

I mean, I've been training for this race for moons. I'm GOOD at Steeplechasing. THE BEST.

Oh, no . . . I have to go. HA is calling me to help her work out what JIMJAMS are.

From which you can deduce that so far
I haven't persuaded her not to sleep over
at Tulip's house. Though I haven't given up
hope that I will.

THE BEST
STEEPLE
CHASER

RUMBLEWICK

Much Later,
So Late It's Nearly Dawning

Dear Diary,

Sadly, I have to report the following:
HA DID go to sleep over with "Tu and Zin"
and I DIDN'T get to enter the Heats because
she WASN'T there to verify that I hadn't
used any magic to make me fly faster.

This is how it went:

I BEGGED
on all fours
for her to attend.

She wasn't interested. "Oh, RB, borrow someone else's witch. Like that old frog-brewer next door . . ."

"She can't," I protested, "she's entering Grimey. And a witch can only vouch for one cat."

"Then find a witch who isn't entering a cat and ask her," HA said. "Anyway, being invited to sleep over at Tu's is the best thing that's ever happened to me, and if you care about me you won't spoil it."

With that,
she was off in her
pink car,

in her JIM wear under
a jam-colored nightgown
(the best we could come up
with for jimjams)
and carrying a toothbrush

of finest elm twigs.

Of course, I should have gone after her.
And deactivated the fly-mode on that car
before she crossed the Horizon.

But I wasn't ready to give up on the
Steeplechase. I fetched my best racing
broomstick and flew to the Clearing
where the Heats start, in the tad of hope
that there was a spare witch
who'd vouch for me.

It was while I was asking around if anyone knew of one that Grimey came rushing up.

"RB, I've been trying to find you to tell you. I was in the Deep Ditch last Ghastly night when the Hags' Familiars were tattlechatting about Haggy Aggy being more Other Side than _This_ Side."

"Tell me something new," I sighed.

"So you know about the GENEROUS REWARD, then?" Grimey whispered. "Being offered by the Hags to anyone who can help CATCH HER IN THE ACT of being more Other Side than This Side?"

YIKES AND TRIPLE YIKES.

My blood froze. My fur stood on end. Pondernot hadn't mentioned A REWARD.

And I could guess why. She didn't
know — because Sassy the Snoop hadn't
told her.

She's kept that part of the tattlechat
to herself because she wants to be the
one who catches HA and claims the

"REWARD"!!

Well, now I had a GIANT problem on my paws, didn't I?

I muttered thanks for the info to Grimey and wished him luck in the Heats.

"You too," he said.

Before I could explain that I wouldn't be taking part, Sassy appeared at my side.

"Rumblewick, hello again!"

she sniggered. "Aren't you entering? Or is your witch too busy — <u>somewhere else</u> — to be here and vouch for you?"

It was a case of SAYING ANYTHING to put her in her place, so I said, "No, Sassy Selfright, she's working on a new collection of New Moon spells. Working so hard she's too busy to be here."

And wished I hadn't.
Because in that tad of trice
Pondernot was beside us
AND SHE HEARD.
  Her face lit up like
the evening star.

'Well, well! My Hagatha, working on a new collection of New Moon spells? How thrillingly willing! How richly witchly! Now, we must make sure the High Hags hear about THIS."

"No!" I squealed like a trapped rat. "No one must know. It's still work-in-secret."

"Oh, but she wouldn't mind me, her dear aunt, having a little preview?" said Pondernot. "It would so lift my spirit to find her reforming in the matter of spell-making and witchly willingness."

So I got tough. I said, glaring mostly at Sassy, "If ANYONE comes snooping before she's ready, HA has told me she will burn the WHOLE COLLECTION."

Tell you more later. HA's come in from her sleepover and she's yelling for me!

HA Bubbles over and the Snoop Comes Snooping

Dear Diary,

Well, in she breezed, kicking off her shoes and bubbling over with excitement.

Of course, first she had to blame me for what HADN'T gone right: why hadn't I told her when you go to a sleepover you don't GO in your sleepover wear? Why hadn't I told her JIM-age girls DON'T DRIVE CARS? Why didn't I tell her that a Mom is only a kind of High Hag but nicer who tells you to go to bed when you want to stay up watching TV?

And why did I give her twigs to clean her teeth and not a BRUSH?

But when she'd gotten all that out, she whipped off her nightgown — revealing herself in a pair of striped shorts and the shortest dress surely ever made — and became sweetness and light.

"Whatever, RB, I forgive you because I had such a superhova time. And look! These are jimjams!"

She twirled round, jumped onto the sofa, and started bouncing on it as she spoke, "Tu gave them to me because I didn't have any and she has seven pairs! Oh, and I learned to giggle which is SO all that. And to bounce on a bed like this a hundred and one times without falling off. And as for sleepover food! You HAVE to taste peanut butter at midnight. AND do you know what? Tu, Zin and me are now so close we're like THIS!"

She twined two fingers round each other and held them up. "And because we're like <u>THIS</u>, I'm invited to sleep over

EVERY

Saturday

until the end

of <u>ever</u>!"

Well, it was another
YIKES AND TRIPLE YIKES moment.
What did she mean "every Saturday
night till the end of ever?" Had she gone
bats on a broomstick in a burning belfry?

I was just considering the kindest way
to tell her she couldn't go sleeping over on
the Other Side AT ALL because the Hags
were after her, when what caught my eye
through the window?

Sassy — on a broomstick — flying
past our house.

Then flying past again and
landing behind the candleberry bushes!!

So, the Snoop had come snooping.

To try and catch

HAGGY AGGY

OUT.

There wasn't a tad of tell to waste. I had to make a plan, triple-presto.

Dear Diary,

I put a plan together

fast enough,

I can tell you.

First I closed the curtains and blocked up all of our thirteen chimneys.

Then I got HA to go to bed — which wasn't hard as, apparently, she hadn't slept a wink at the sleepover.

While she slept, I wrote a note to Tu and Zin in Otherside handwriting, which thankfully I had learned so well at school.

Here is a copy:

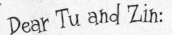

Dear Tu and Zin:

For your information Aggy is not what she seems.
She is not a girl jimmer. She is A WITCH. A true
and proper witch even if she doesn't always behave
like one. Believe me, I am a highly trained Witch's
Familiar and I know.

So if you are horrified — which you should
be — and do not want a witch in your JIM class or
at your sleepovers, my advice is BANISH HER

AT THE FIRST OPPORTUNITY.

Yours truly,

I'd better not give my name.

PS: If you don't believe me take a look in your garden.
All the witch's artifacts you find there are HERS.

PPS: It will be best if you do not tell her you received this
warning. Just say "you guessed" because of her supernova
JIM — which, by the way, has all been mightily spelled.

Next I filled two large ingredient-collecting bags with the following:

One foldaway broomstick
One porta-cauldron
One full witch's all-black
outfit, including hat
Three jars of allspell ingredients —
dried slug slime, blagwort
seeds, weasel earwax.

With the bags astraddle my broomstick —
and the Note safely tucked under my
hat — I flew off toward the Tanglewoods,
which are well-known collecting grounds.
So if Sassy was watching from behind the
candleberry bushes, she wouldn't think I was up to
anything unusual.

Once I was sure she wasn't following me, I changed direction and sped back over the Horizon to Tu's house. (Luckily I'd found her address under HA's pillow.)

Here I placed the contents of my bags in a convenient garden shed and pushed THE NOTE through Tu's bedroom window.

To be sure she got the message, I waited and watched until I saw her pick it up and read it!

Now all I had to do was get HA to one last JIM class — where SURELY Tu would say, "ZIN and I DO NOT want a WITCH for a BEST FRIEND or bouncing with us on our very own beds in our very own houses. SO GO HOME, WITCH, AND STAY THERE."

And that would be the end of that. There'd be no more Otherside sleeping over for Sassy to catch her at!!

Brilliant, if I do say so myself.

My Brilliant Plan Continues

Dear Diary,

As I arrived home, I saw Sassy in the bushes covered in chimney soot!! Good, I thought, try all thirteen chimneys. You won't get in that way. You won't get in any way. Because you won't be going anywhere. Especially, you won't be following HA to her last and all-important JIM class where — if everything goes according to my plan — she is going to be UNbefriended by her new, best, Otherside sleepover friends.

And so, the next day while HA was putting on her JIM wear, I grounded that selfrighting Snooper in the REAL sense of the word:

THE FAILPROOF-GROUNDING SPELL

Crush an old unflyable broomstick to dust and mix with pressed pine gum. Fly over the One to Be Grounded, sprinkling the mixture and chanting:

Wherever you wish to go
Wherever you wish to linger
You cannot move a foot
A paw or little finger
Wherever you wish to sneak
Whether it's near or far
The very ground you stand on
Holds you where you are!

SMALL PRINT: This spell is failproof unless the One Being Spelled uses a spell to override it within two tads of tell of it being performed on him/her/it.

And, as Sassy wasn't expecting it, she didn't have an overrider ready to override it. So there she was —

ACTUALLY STUCK IN THE MUD —

in her Snoop's hideout behind the

candleberry bushes!!!

My Brilliant Plan Backfires

Dear Diary,

So that the grounded Sassy wouldn't look up and see HA flying off in JIM clothes, I offered to take her to the class myself — provided she <u>COVER HERSELF UP</u> in a cloak and hat.

I said there was a chill wind blowing and she wouldn't want to catch cold and not be at her best. She agreed without a fight, though with lots of moaning that I fuss too much.

Whatever, I didn't care. I was just relieved to deliver her to the door of the JIM building for what I felt certain was

THE BEGINNING OF THE END OF OTHERSIDE <u>SLEEPING OVER</u>.

ONLY,

IT DID NOT
WORK OUT

LIKE THAT
AT ALL.

"RB," she crowed, as I picked her up afterward, "Tu and Zin are SO EXCITED about having me for a best friend, they're asking all their other friends to the sleepover this Saturday night. To show me off! Now what am I going to WEAR for this SHOW-ME-OFF party?"

So excited?
About having A WITCH for a friend??
Talk about a plan backfiring.
I mean,
what were those
girls thinking of,
and now what???

The Grounding spell keeping Sassy stuck in the mud will have worn off by "Saturday" night. She'll be on

A RAMPAGE OF REVENGE!!

(And no doubt ready with an overrider in case I try to ground her again!)

Besides — and it's a GIANT BESIDES — this "Saturday" night is the night of the actual Steeplechase Race.

Everyone will be there.

EVERY WITCH AND EVERY FAMILIAR.

If HA isn't, the High Hags will WANT TO KNOW WHERE SHE IS.

And if the Snoop follows HA to Tu's, which she will, she'll be able to lead the Hags straight to her.

HA will be caught in the Act and Sassy will claim the Reward.

And here's the thing, Diary —
SNOOPING will have won.
So I better get rethinking because

I'M NOT HAVING THAT!

"Saturday" Night — Nearly Dawning

Dear Diary,

I thought and rethought. The best I could come up with was to tell HA about the danger she was in.

But when I did she just brushed it all aside.

"Oh RB, let the Snoops snoop, let the Hags catch. Let them have their rewards. My reward — being shown off at a sleepover — is far the greater!"

"But what about ME," I begged. "If you're caught at Tu's, I'll get the blame for letting you go — and probably sent back to Awethunder's to relearn my lessons!"

"Oh, those old Hags are so full of hot soup." She laughed.

"They won't send you back to school — there aren't enough Familiars to go around as it is. So stop fretting!"

I shot my last arrow.

"Well, what about Pondernot? Think how RUBBLEROT she's going to make you feel."

"She won't get the chance," HA laughed, "as I'll NEVER drop in on her again!"

And that was that.

Haggy Aggy went to the sleepover. Not even covered up in a cloak and hat. Completely UNAWARE that Tu knows she is a witch because her Familiar (YOURS TRULY, ME) has told her. And with Sassy the Snoop certain to be following her!!!

YIKES AND TRIPLE YIKES! I had to face it: WHAT A GROTTLEPOTCH I WAS MAKING OF THIS.

So after moping about for some tads of tell, I decided I had no choice.

I had to go after HA on my own broomstick [1] to confess what I'd done and [2] to keep a lookout for Sassy.

Several times as I flew I thought I saw her and went in hot pursuit — only to find I was chasing shadows.

As a result, by the time I arrived at Tu's — and took up my observation post in a tree — the sleepover was in full swing.

Though, of course, not at all as HA was expecting.

Tu, Zin and "all their friends" were dragging her to the garden shed screaming,

"Come on, Aggy. Put on your witch's stuff. Show us how you ride a **broomstick!**"

"What do you mean?" HA gulped. "What witch's stuff? I am not a witch. What makes you think I am?"

"We guessed!" cried Zin. "From your JIM! Which is so magic you must be one!" They pushed her into the shed yelling,

"PUT IT ALL ON.
THEN RIDE YOUR BROOMSTICK.
WE LOVE WITCHES."

After a lot of thunderous snarling from inside, the shed door opened and HA emerged — in the black clothing I'd put there and holding the broomstick.

"Ride, ride!"
cried Tulip.
"Show us how you do it."

HA turned green.

But she got astride the broomstick, shot up in the air, circled twice, and landed proudly — without so much as a double foot brake.

Now Tu and Zin begged to be taken up for rides.

How could HA say no to her best friends who were so close they were "entwined"?

Looking even greener, she took them each up for a spin.

Then, because the girl begged so hard, she took up one of the "other friends." And I could see exactly what she was trying to do.

Buck her off!

At the same tad of tell I saw something else I'd rather I hadn't: the unmistakable shape of a Familiar on a broom against the moon.

Sassy!

My heart sank and then sank deeper when I realized the shape was heading AWAY from us.

She'd already been and seen and was no doubt flying back to tell the Hags where they could find HA being shown off by Otherside friends at an

Otherside

sleepover

party!!

Now what?

Go after her and stop her?

Or save an unwitting

girl-child

from being

bucked off
a broomstick?

The girl started to fall. There was nothing else to do. I swooped out and caught her neatly on the back of my broomstick.

But this only got me <u>more</u> into boil and bubble and no closer to going after Sassy.

HA was furious to find me there. Especially when the girls crowded around and made a huge fuss of M<u>E</u>!

"Thank you and enough," she snapped.

"I don't know who this cat is or w<u>hat</u> it's doing here.

Let's watch TV."

"TV!?" cried Tulip.

"Who wants to watch TV when there's a **real witch** and her **cat** to play with!

And now we want you to make us a real spell."

Zin dragged the porta-cauldron out of the shed.

"Make us a spell to turn all the girls we don't like at school INTO SLIMY TOADS."

Tulip presented HA with a basket. "We've collected ingredients. All the horrid things you witches put in spells."

And suddenly I saw ALL WAS NOT LOST.

The basket was full of everything HA loves to protect:

frogs, snails, a bat, a jar of newts, and a terrified shrew.

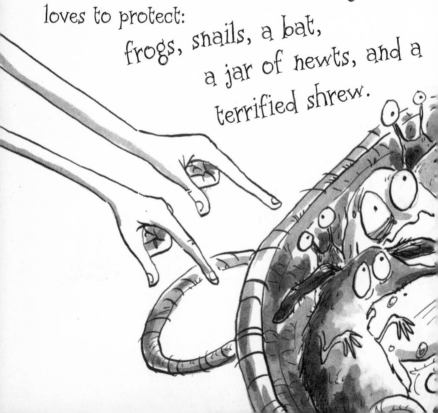

Little did those girls know how the idea of using them would upset HA.

As they shrieked and demanded their spell, I could see a full-on witch's fit brewing.

"A spell!" she cried, going puce. "Using these dear living creatures? To turn girls you don't like into toads?

We'll see about that!!"

She grabbed the ingredients I'd put in the shed, flew up on her broomstick, and sprinkled the girls with them, chanting:

Ghastly girls who are not kind
In this moment we will find
You're frogs and snails, you're bats, a shrew
Not living — that's too good for you
So wish you'd watched TV with me

FOR GARDEN ORNAMENTS YOU BE!

And — since she is a great witch when she's willing — immediately those girls were STONE.

Then yelling at me to join HER on her broomstick, she set off at the speed of lightness for This Side!!

And all I can say is: was our luck in or what?

We were just back over the Horizon when we met the Hags — being led by the Snoop and making for Tulip's — to catch HA IN THE ACT!

Instead,
they found
us together on
a broomstick, as we
should be, HA flying it in
top-to-toe black.

As they stopped, in surprise, I called out,
"Evening, Your Hagships. Going to the Other
Side, are you? Well, while there, go to
House Number 5, Partridge Close, and check
out one of Hagatha's New Moon spells. And
for your info, those garden ornaments were
all once GIRLS."

"And they will be again, when the spell
wears off," called HA, "only wiser for the
experience!"

The Hags spluttered — while Sassy went
into such a spin of disappointment, she
actually fell off her broomstick!! And HA
did the last thing I was expecting.

She called out: "Well, we can't hang around up here. We must get over to the Steeplechase!"

And, knock me over with a dandelion, she added, "Oh, and by the way, Amuletta. Rumblewick MUST be allowed to race even if he did miss the Heats.

And if you won't let him,

I'll turn you into a MOM!"

Well, clearly Amuletta didn't want to run that risk, because I did get to race.

And, as I am the best, I WAS the best and won — and have the trophy to prove it!!

Better still — Sassy didn't even make the race. When she fell off her broomstick, we were over the Tanglewoods. Of course, she wouldn't have come to any harm because — like name, like nature — she could right herself even if she fell off the evening star.

But here's the thing: it takes almost a moon to walk it back to ANYWHERE from the Tanglewoods.

So all I can say to Sassy is — you got your just reward, Snoop . . .

AND KEEP WALKING!

WITCHES' CHARTER
OF GOOD PRACTICE

1. Scare at least one child on the Other Side
into his or her wits — every day (excellent),
once in seven days (good), once a moon (average),
once in two moons (bad), once in a blue
moon (failed).

2. Identify any fully grown Othersiders
who were not properly scared into their wits as
children and DO IT NOW. (It is never too
late for a grown Othersider to come to
his or her senses.)

3. Invent a new spell useful for every purpose
and every occasion in the Witches' Calendar.
Ensure you or your Familiar commits it to
a spell book before it is lost to the
Realms of Forgetfulness forever.

4. Keep a proper witch's house at all
times — filled with dust and spiders' webs, mold,
and earwigs' underthings; and ensure the jars on
your kitchen shelves are always alive with
good spell ingredients.

5. Cackle a lot. Cackling can be heard far and wide and serves many purposes such as (i) alerting others to your terrifying presence and (ii) sounding hideous and thereby comforting to your fellow witches.

6. Make sure your Familiar keeps your means of proper travel (broomsticks) in good repair and that one, either, or both of you exercise them regularly.

7. Never fail to present yourself anywhere and everywhere in full witch's uniform (i.e., black everything and no ribbons upon your hat ever). Sleeping in uniform is recommended as a means of saving dressing time.

8. Keep your Familiar happy with a good supply of comfrey tea and slime buns. Remember, behind every great witch is a well-fed Familiar.

9. At all times acknowledge the authority of your local High Hags. As their eyes can move 360 degrees and they know everything there is to know, it is always in your interests to make their wishes your commands.

Can't get enough of Rumblewick's diaries? Check out
My Unwilling Witch Starts a Girl Band

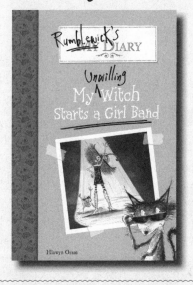

available
November 2009

Here's a note from
Rumblewick about
Haggy Aggy's
latest antics:

Dear Reader,

HA's nearly driving me over the edge and into the cauldron! She doesn't want to behave like a proper witch and fly her broom or practice her cackle—she wants to be a STAR. Haggy Aggy is dead-set on entering the Girl Bands Are Us contest and becoming a magma-hot rocker. But how am I to stop her and avoid the wrath of the High Hags if I can't stop my head from ting-zinging and my paws from tap-rapping along with the music? Am I starstruck, or what?

Want to hear more about my daily trials and tribulations with the only witch in witchdom who doesn't want to be one? I've described more in this diary....

TURN THE PAGE FOR A SNEAK PEEK!

Very sincerely,

Rumblewick Spellwacker Mortimer B.

Dear Diary,

What a day it has been at The Righton.

After a stare-filled lunch (well, HA's hat WAS bigger than an alien wizard's flying saucer), she was attracted by a sign near the hotel entrance. "Oh, RB!" she cried. "Do look! It's covered in glitzy stars so it must have something very important to communicate. Now you read Otherside better than I do, so read it to me, _please,_

at the triple pr_esto!_"

So I did and in between the STARS it said:

GIRL BANDS ARE US

WE MAKE THEM **BIG.**
COULD YOU BE OUR NEXT
BIG ONE?
AUDITIONS START AT 3 PM
IN THE STARSTRUCK ROOM
ON THE FIRST FLOOR.
BE THERE AND BE **BIGGER THAN**
YOU **EVER DREAMED**
YOU COULD BE.

At that point we did not know what
a Girl Band or a Girl Band audition was
but HA insisted we go up to the
Starstruck Room to find out.

And find out we did: a Girl Band is
Otherside girls dressing up (or
wearing clothes that nearly fall off),
dancing on a shiny platform and
singing like their voices just jumped
out of their bodies and got dancing too.

An audition is when a Girl Band
does all the above in front of three
Othersiders who are called the Producers
and Promoters.

When the PPs have watched many Girl
Band auditions over many moons, they
will choose the band they like best and
make it "bigger" than it
ever dreamed it could be.

And being **bigger** than you ever

dreamed

you could be means

1 dancing and singing on TV and shiny platforms all over the universe,

2️⃣ having zillions of your songs heard by Othersiders in what they call ALBUMS,

20 Zillion Album Sales

3️⃣ appearing on pocket-sized TVs that Othersiders keep close at all times (and also use for nonstop stalking to OTHER Othersiders probably because they don't have broomsticks to get there and talk for real).

Well, no prizes for guessing what HA is going to do now.

Oh YES!

The moment we left the Starstruck Room, she announced it.

She is going to start her own Girl Band.
And enter it in the next

GIRL BANDS
ARE US

audition in seven days' time!!

WARNING
TOP
SECRET

And here, dear
Diary, is where I am
going to make a CONFESSION because
that's what diaries are for — admitting the
secret thoughts you can't actually admit to
anyone else.

So this is it.
My secret confession:
I LIKE GIRL BAND
MUSIC.

Up there in the
Starstruck Room it
got me going — my
head ting-zinging and my paws tap-rapping.
   And when my witch announced she was
going to start a Girl Band, I did not think
YUKSTRAW and TRIPLE YIKES, which any
proper Witch's Familiar should think.

I thought EXPLODING SUPERNOVAS and OVER THE MOON. THIS COULD BOIL AND BUBBLE!

Naturally, I did not admit any of this to HA. When we got back to our room, I did what I am trained to do when my witch strays from being a proper witch. I tried to talk her out of it.

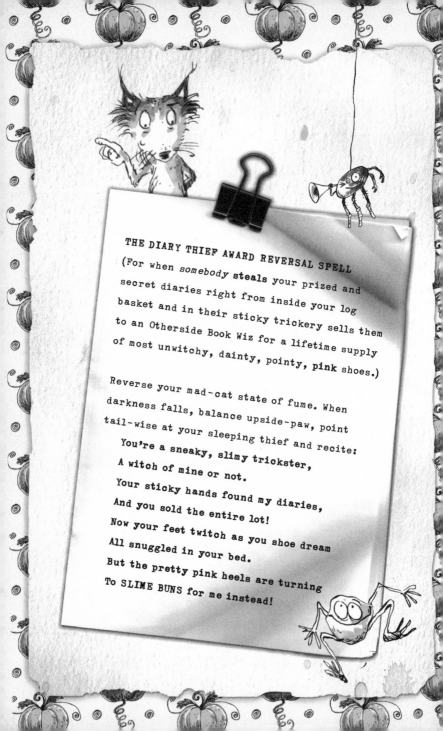

THE DIARY THIEF AWARD REVERSAL SPELL
(For when *somebody* **steals** your prized and
secret diaries right from inside your log
basket and in their sticky trickery sells them
to an Otherside Book Wiz for a lifetime supply
of most unwitchy, dainty, pointy, **pink** shoes.)

Reverse your mad-cat state of fume. When
darkness falls, balance upside-paw, point
tail-wise at your sleeping thief and recite:

   You're a sneaky, slimy trickster,
   A witch of mine or not.
   Your sticky hands found my diaries,
   And you sold the entire lot!
   Now your feet twitch as you shoe dream
   All snuggled in your bed.
   But the pretty pink heels are turning
   To SLIME BUNS for me instead!

Hello, this is the Publisher's Familiar here. Since our last interview with Rumblewick Spellwacker Mortimer B, this wise and witty Otherside phenom has been world-trotting and hot-rocking. Once again, the fantastic feline sat down with Yours Truly to discuss broomstick bucking, the wizardry of girl band lyrics, and his hatred of Otherside food.

PUBLISHER'S FAMILIAR: How did you know that Familiar-ism was the job for you?

RUMBLEWICK: I come from a long line of highly qualified witch's Familiars. My parents were both famous Familiars in their day and took me to work with them from when I was knee high to a cauldron leg. So there was never a question of doing anything else.

PF: But if you *weren't* a Familiar, what else would you like to be doing?

RB: Well, unless the High Hags send me spinning into The Blue Beyond the Blue and/or I get catnapped by Alien Wizards and turned into a Space Time Serf, I won't be giving up Familiar-ing in any of my lives. But I don't mind mentioning I am rather brilliantly starry at writing song lyrics and wearing dark shades as discovered when Haggy Aggy tried to start her own Girl Band and asked me to be its manager. So, if I wasn't what I am and always will be, I'd get mixed up in foot-tapping, hot-bop, and rocking music.

PF: And are you still bound to Haggy Aggy, or are your terms of contract null and void upon your famousness?

RB: N.O. spells no in this case. The High Hags, who rule and drew up my contract, ignore my famousdom on the Other Side and continue pointing their pointing fingers at me as if it is my fault Haggy Aggy wants to be anything and everything in the universe except what she is—a witch.

PF: How difficult is it to maneuver a broomstick? How long did it take you to learn to fly?

RB: I was riding a broomstick before I could walk. To maneuver well, you have to have a relationship with the sticks. Trim them, tune them, talk to them and keep them warm. And always warn them of an upcoming turn, well in advance, or don't be surprised if you're free-falling. You'll just have been BUCKED.

PF: Haggy Aggy's desires have you traveling across the Horizon Line quite often. What is your favorite thing about the Other Side?

RB: Certainly NOT the food which is total GRUB-SPIT and GRUMSPEW for no matter how hard you look you can't get a single Slime Bun, Fleabane Finger, Wig-You-Not Lushti or Begone Berry Nugget — NOT ANY-WHERE AT ALL. What I suppose I *do* like, aside from hot-rocking girl bands, are the ratlets that they call children over there. When it comes down to it, they and I have a lot in common. They have to think on their feet (since they don't have paws, worst luck for them), be inventive in the face of high disappointment, keep out of the Abyss of Trouble, avoid the Narrow Avoid and not let *their* High Hags — whoever they are — hang them over a hot cauldron till their hair curls.

Dear Precious Children,

The Publisher asked me to say something about these Diaries.
(As I do not write Otherside very well, I have dictated it to
the Publisher's Familiar/assistant. If she has not written it
down right, let me know and I'll turn her into a fat pumpkin.)

This is my message: I went to a lot of trouble to steal these
Diaries for you. And the Publisher gave me a lot of shoes
in exchange. If you do not read them the Publisher may
want the shoes back. So please, for my sake — the only
witch in witchdom who isn't willing to scare you for her own
entertainment — ENJOY THEM ALL.

Yours ever,

Haggy Aggy

Your fantabulous shoe-loving friend,
Hagatha Agatha (Haggy Aggy for short, HA for shortest) xx

NORMAL PUBLIC LIBRARY
NORMAL, ILLINOIS 617